This book was a
gift to Butterfield
School Library to
honor the birthday of

Anna Groebe

February 28, 1991

MARC BROWN

ARTHUR'S APRIL FOOL

Little, Brown and Company
BOSTON   NEW YORK   TORONTO   LONDON

Library of Congress Cataloging in Publication Data

Brown, Marc Tolon.
  Arthur's April fool.

  Summary: Arthur worries about remembering his magic
tricks for the April Fool's Day assembly and Binky's
threats to pulverize him.
  [1. April Fool's Day—Fiction. 2. Magic tricks—
Fiction. 3. Bullies—Fiction] I. Title.
PZ7.B81618Ao 1983   [E]   82-20368
ISBN 0-316-11196-1
ISBN 0-316-11234-8 (pbk.)

HC: 20 19 18 17 16 15 14 13 12 11
PB: 20 19 18 17 16 15 14 13 12

It was the last day of March.
The joke shop was full of people getting
ready for April Fool's Day.
Arthur and Buster tried out everything.
Buster bought sneezing powder.
Arthur got a fake telescope that gave
whoever looked through it a black eye.
But Arthur didn't feel like playing jokes.
He kept thinking about Binky Barnes.
"Who is Binky Barnes?" asked Buster.
"Picture King Kong. Now double it,"
said Arthur. "He keeps threatening
to punch me out."

Later that day, Arthur was practicing his
magic tricks with Buster and Francine
for the April Fool's assembly.
"Hey, shrimp!"
A giant shadow covered them.
"I'll show *you* a trick," said Binky Barnes.
He grabbed Arthur's favorite pen
and put it in his pocket.

"Now you see it, now you don't," said Binky.
"Hey, watch it," said Arthur, trying to look brave.
"Why don't you make me," said Binky,
and walked away.
"Pick on someone your own size,"
called Francine. "Like Godzilla!"
"Wow," said Buster, "you were right.
He's going to pulverize you!"

That night at dinner Arthur hardly ate anything.
He didn't finish his cheeseburger.
He didn't even want any chocolate cream pie.
"What's the matter with Arthur?" asked his father.
"He's worried about getting pulverized," said D.W.
"Maybe he's been watching too many
outer space movies," said his mother.

Later on, D.W. barged into Arthur's room.
"Good night, Mr. Universe," she said.
"Haven't you ever heard of knocking?" asked Arthur.
"After you get pulverized, can I
have your room?" she asked.
"Beat it, D.W."

When Arthur finally fell asleep,
he had nightmares.

The next morning, Francine offered Arthur a cookie.
"Yuk!" said Arthur.
"This tastes like soap and toothpaste."
"April Fool!" laughed Francine.
But Arthur was too worried to laugh.
"I'll never remember my magic tricks
for the assembly," he said.

"Calm down," said Buster. "I'll be your assistant.
I'll help if you get stuck."
Arthur felt better. He could count on Buster.
But just before the assembly Buster got caught
putting sneezing powder on Mr. Ratburn's desk.
Instead of going to the assembly,
Buster went to the principal's office.

"I'll blow it for sure without Buster,"
thought Arthur.
He walked into the auditorium.
Who was sitting in the front row?
Binky Barnes.
This was going to be even worse than he thought.

Arthur worried while Mr. Ratburn
read people's minds.

He worried while Francine
and Muffy did shadow tricks.

And he worried while the chorus sang
"That Old Black Magic."
Finally, it was his turn.

"For my first trick," said Arthur,
"I'll need a volunteer . . ."
Binky Barnes jumped on the stage.
"Surprise, pipsqueak!" he whispered.
Arthur gulped.

Arthur asked Binky Barnes to tear up
a sheet of paper and put it in the magic hat.
He said the magic words and waved
his magic wand to make the paper whole again.

But rabbits came out instead.
Everyone laughed.
Arthur took a bow.
By mistake, flowers fell out of his sleeve.
Binky Barnes laughed harder than anyone.

Then Arthur had an idea.
He winked at Francine.
"For my next trick I will saw
this young man in half."
Binky stopped laughing and took a step back.
"My saw, please," said Arthur.
Binky turned pale.

"And now the bucket to collect the blood."
Binky screamed.
He stepped back again, this time
right off the stage.
Everyone laughed, even Mr. Ratburn.

After the assembly Arthur stopped Binky in the hall.

"What's the matter, Binky? You left
before I could show you my best trick."
"No thanks," said Binky Barnes.
"Are you sure? It lets you see things
you've never seen before," said Arthur.
"Really?" said Binky.

He grabbed the telescope
and pointed it at Francine.
"I don't see anything."
"Of course not," said Arthur.
"You have to know the secret words."

"Tell me!" said Binky.
"I can't," Arthur explained. "They're so
secret I have to write them down — backwards.
Do you have a pen?"
"Sure, here," said Binky.
Arthur wrote the words.
"Now go home, hold the paper up to the mirror,
and you'll be able to read the secret words."
"Thanks, twerp," said Binky
as he ran out the door.

"Boy, that's your best trick yet," said Buster.
"You didn't get pulverized and
you made Binky Barnes disappear."
"What did you write?" asked Francine.